The Table Where
Rich People Sit

The Table Where Rich People Sit

Byrd Baylor • Pictures by Peter Parnall

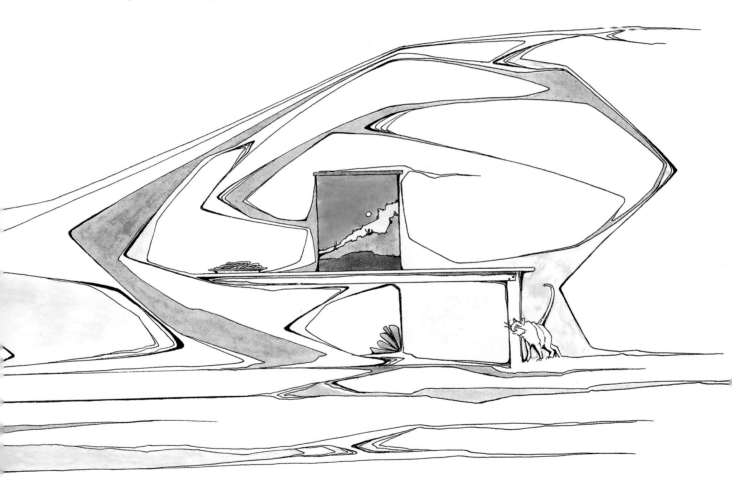

Aladdin Paperbacks

First Aladdin Paperbacks edition July 1998

Text copyright © 1994 by Byrd Baylor
Illustrations copyright © 1994 by Peter Parnall

Aladdin Paperbacks
An imprint of Simon & Schuster Children's Publishing Division
1230 Avenue of the Americas
New York, NY 10020

The Library of Congress has cataloged the hardcover edition as follows:
Baylor, Byrd.
The table where rich people sit / Byrd Baylor : pictures by Peter Parnall. — 1st. ed.
p.   cm.
Summary: A girl discovers that her impoverished family is rich in things that matter in life,
especially being outdoors and experiencing nature.
ISBN 0-684-19653-0
[1. Wealth—Fiction. 2. Nature—Fiction. 3. Family life—Fiction.]
I. Parnall, Peter, ill. II. Title.
PZ7.B3435Tab   1994   [E]—dc20   93-1251
ISBN 0-689-82008-9 (pbk.)

For Jesse

If you could see us
sitting here
at our old,
scratched-up,
homemade
kitchen table,
you'd know that
we aren't rich.

But my father
is trying to tell us
we *are*.

Doesn't he notice
my worn-out shoes?
Or that my little brother
has patches
on the pants he wears
to first grade?
And why does he think
that old rattletrap truck
is parked by our door?

"You can't fool me,"
 I say.
"We're *poor*.
 Would rich people sit
 at a table
 like this?"

My mother
sort of pats
the table
and she says,
"Well, we're rich
 and we sit here
 every day."

Sometimes
I think
that I'm the only one
in my whole family
who is really
sensible.

Maybe I should mention
that my parents
made this table
out of lumber
somebody else
threw away.
They even had a celebration
when they finished it.

Understand,
I like this table
fine.
All I'm saying is,
you can tell
it didn't come
from a furniture store.
It just doesn't look
like a table where
rich people
would sit.

But my mother thinks
if all the rulers of the world
could get together
at a friendly wooden table
in somebody's kitchen,
they would solve
their arguments
in half the time.

And my father says
it wouldn't hurt
to have a lot of cookies
piled up on a nice blue plate
that everyone could reach
without asking.

But tonight
it's *our* kitchen
and *our* argument
and *our* family meeting
and *our* very spicy ginger cookies
piled up on my mother's
one good blue-flowered plate
exactly
in the center of the table.

I'm the one
who called the meeting,
and the subject is
money;
and I say we don't have
enough
of it.

I tell my parents
they should both get
better jobs
so we could buy
a lot of
nice new things.
I tell them
I look worse
than anyone
in school.

"I hate to bring this up,"
I say,
"but it would help
if you both had
a little more
ambition."

They look surprised.
You can see
they never think about
the things we need.

Right here,
I might as well admit
that my parents have
some strange ideas
about
working.

They think
the only jobs worth having
are jobs
outdoors.

They want cliffs
or canyons
or desert
or mountains
around them
wherever they work.
They even want a good view
of the sky.

They always work together,
and their favorite thing
is panning gold—
piling us into that beat-up truck
and heading for
the rocky desert hills
or back in some narrow
mountain gully
where all the roads
are just coyote trails.

They love to walk
the wide arroyos,
the dry streambeds,
where little flecks of gold
are found.
They used to tell us that
the truck just knew
which roads to take
and that coyotes showed them
where to look for gold—
but I never did believe it.

After a month or two out there,
they always had
a little bit of gold to sell,
but you can tell
it never made them rich.

As far as I can see,
it was just an excuse
to camp
in some beautiful
wild place
again.

They don't mind
planting fields of
sweet corn or alfalfa.
They like to pick chile
and squash and tomatoes.
They'll put up strong fences
or train wild young horses.

But they say
they
can't stand
to be cooped up
indoors.

So now, of course,
my dad is asking,
"How many people
are as lucky as we are?"

But I've called this meeting
and I say,
"I bet you could make more money
working in a building
somewhere
in town."

"Remember our
number one rule,"
he says.
"We have to see the sky."

"You could look
through
a window,"
I say.

But they won't even
think
about it.

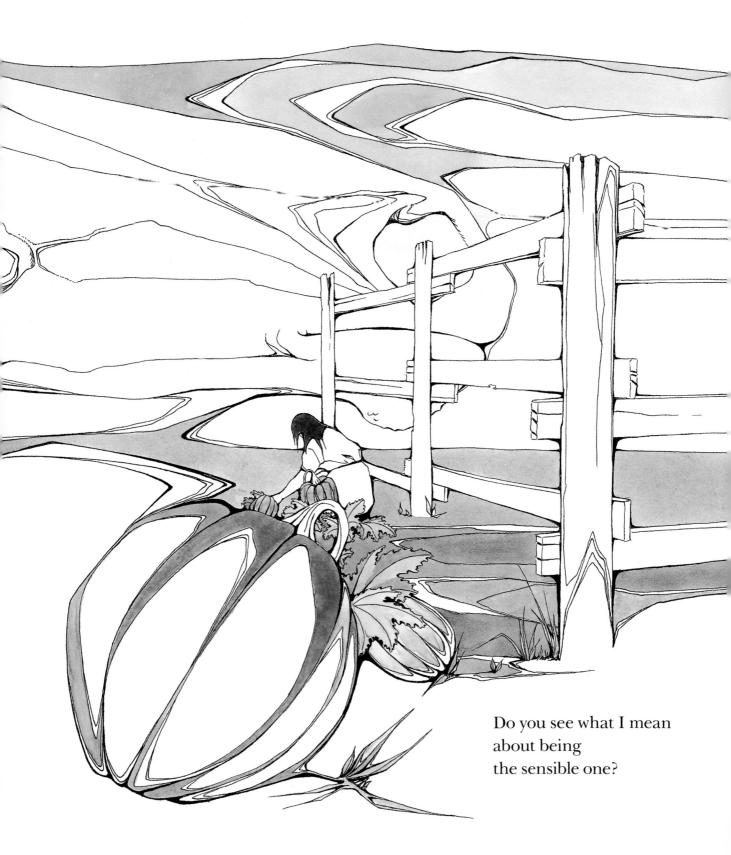

Do you see what I mean
about being
the sensible one?

Finally, my mother says,
"All right, Mountain Girl.
We're going to explain
how we figure our money.
You be the bookkeeper
tonight."

She hands us each
a pencil
and some yellow paper.
She gives some
to my little brother, too,
though he'll just sit there
pretending to write
when we write,
or he'll draw people dancing
up in the sky.

And by the way,
my name's not really
Mountain Girl.

They call me that
because I was born
in a cabin
on the side of a mountain
where they were looking
for gold
one summertime
in Arizona.

They say
it was the most
magical place,
the most beautiful
mountain
they ever climbed.
Maybe it was,
but you know how
those two
exaggerate.

Anyway,
they wanted
my first sight
to be that mountainside,
so they held me up
outdoors
at sunrise
when I was just about
eight minutes old.

The truth is,
I still like sunrise
quite a lot.

And my little brother. . .
They call him
Ocean Boy.
They say
since I already had
the best mountain
for my first sight,
they thought
they ought to find
the most beautiful ocean
for him.
I think they went
all over Mexico
looking for a place
where ocean touches jungle.
And they had to find
a certain kind of
purple-blue night sky
and the exact
green waves
they like.

They held him up
to see those waves
for his first sight.

Someday
we're all going back
to his green ocean
and my high mountain.
But for now
(even though they claim
to be so rich)
they can't take us
anywhere
at all.

No wonder
I had to call this meeting
about money.

Can you believe
my father is
sitting here
looking me straight in the eye
and saying,
"But, Mountain Girl,
I thought you knew
how rich we are."

I say,
"We can't get very far
in this discussion
if you won't even admit
that we're poor."

"I'll prove it to you
right now,"
he says.
"Let's make a list
of the money we earn
in a year."

"How much is that?"
I ask.
"I'll write it down."

But he says,
"Not so fast.
We have a lot of things
to think about
before we add them up."

"What kinds of things?"

My mother says,
"We don't just
take our pay
in cash,
you know.
We have a special plan
so we get paid
in sunsets, too,
and in having time
to hike around
the canyons
and look for eagle nests."

But I say,
"Can't you give me
one single number
to write down
on this paper?"

So we start with
twenty thousand dollars.

That's how much
my father says
it's worth to him
to work outdoors,
where he can see sky
all day
and feel the wind
and smell rain
an hour before
it's really raining.

He says it's worth
that much
to be where
(if he feels like singing)
he can sing out loud
and no one will mind.

I have just written
twenty thousand
when my mother says,
"You'd better make that
thirty thousand
because
it's worth at least
another *ten*
to hear coyotes
howling
back in the hills."

So I write
thirty thousand.

Then she remembers that
they like to see
long distances
and faraway mountains
that change color
about ten times a day.

"That's worth another
five thousand dollars to me,"
she says.

I'm not surprised
because my mother
claims to be
an expert
on mountain shadows
in the desert.
She says
she can tell time
by the way
those colors change
from dawn to dark.

I scratch out what I had
and write
thirty-five thousand dollars.

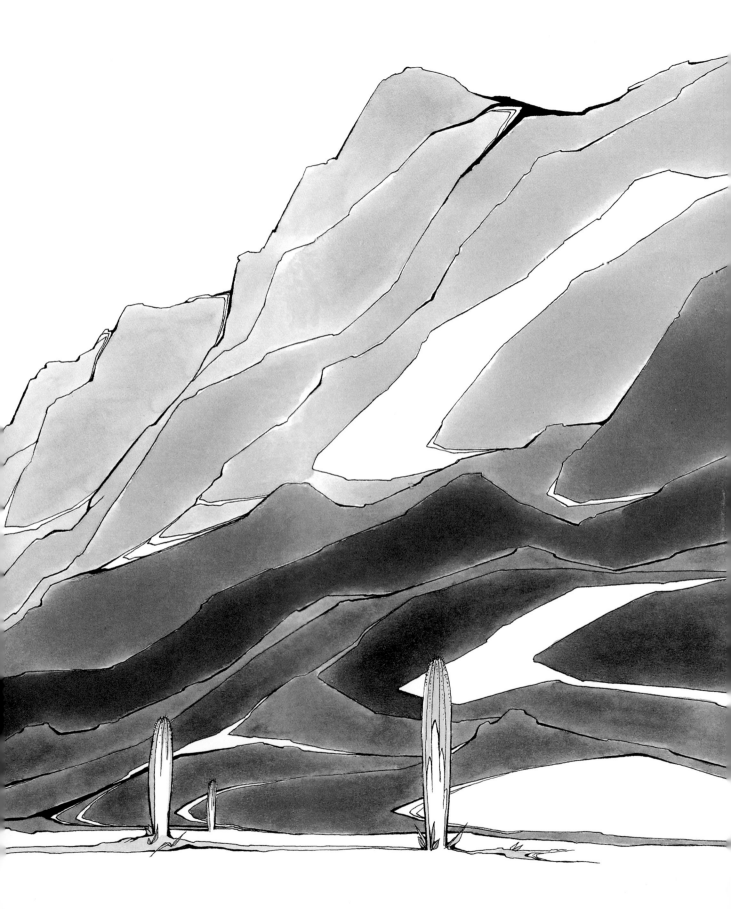

My father thinks of
something else.
"When a cactus blooms,
you should be there
to watch it
because
it might be a color
you won't see again
any other day
of your life.
How much would you say
that color is worth?"

"Fifty cents?"
my brother asks.

But they decide on
another
five thousand.

So now I write
forty thousand dollars.

But I'd forgotten
how much my father likes
to make bird sounds.
He can copy any bird,
but he's best at
white-winged doves
and ravens and red-tailed hawks
and quail.
He's good at eagles, too,
and great horned owls.
So, of course,
he has to add
another ten thousand
for having
both day birds and night birds
around us.

I cross out what I had
and I write
fifty thousand dollars.

Now my mother says,
"Let's see what
our Mountain Girl
is worth to us."

I'm beginning to catch on
to their kind of thinking,
so I suggest
I'm worth
ten thousand dollars
even though my little brother
has begun to laugh.

"Don't underestimate yourself,"
my father says.
"Remember all those good lists
you make for us."

He's right. I do.
I made a list of the best books
each one of us has read
and a list of all the ones
we want to read again.
I also made a list
of all the animals
each one of us has seen
and the ones we still
most want to see
out in the wild—
not in a zoo.

Mine is a mountain lion.
I've dreamed of him four times,
and I've already seen
his track.
My father chose
a grizzly bear.
My mother wants to see
a wolf
and hear it call.
And my brother
can't decide
between a dolphin
and a whale.
I remember every one
because
I make the lists.

They end up deciding
I'm worth about
a million dollars.

I say I don't think
I am,
but I write it anyway.

In fact, it turns out
that every one of us
is worth a million.

So we have
four million
and fifty thousand dollars.

Then I realize
I want to add
five thousand dollars
myself
for the pleasure I have
wandering
in open country,
alone,
free as a lizard,
not following trails,
not having a plan,
just turning
whatever way
the wind turns me.

They say
that's certainly worth
five thousand.

So that makes
*four million
and fifty-five thousand dollars.*

Finally,
my brother says
to put down
seven dollars more
for all the nights
we get to sleep
outside
under the stars.

We all say
seven dollars
doesn't seem to be
enough.
We talk him into
making it
five thousand.

Now my paper says
*four million
and sixty thousand dollars*—
and we haven't even started
counting
actual cash.

To tell the truth,
the cash part
doesn't seem to matter
anymore.

I suggest
it shouldn't even be
on a list
of our kind of
riches.

So the meeting is over.

The rest of them
have gone outside
to see the new
sliver of moon.
But I'm still
sitting here
at our nice
homemade
kitchen table
with one cookie left
on my mother's
good blue-
flowered plate,
and
I'm writing
this book
about us.

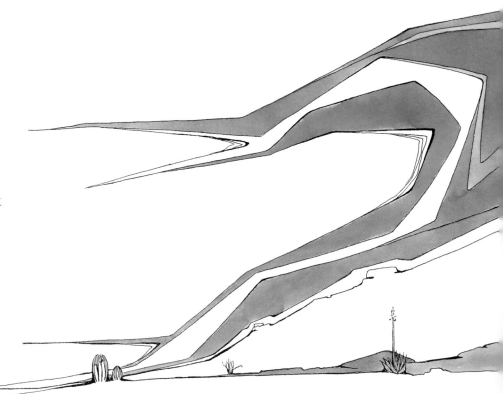

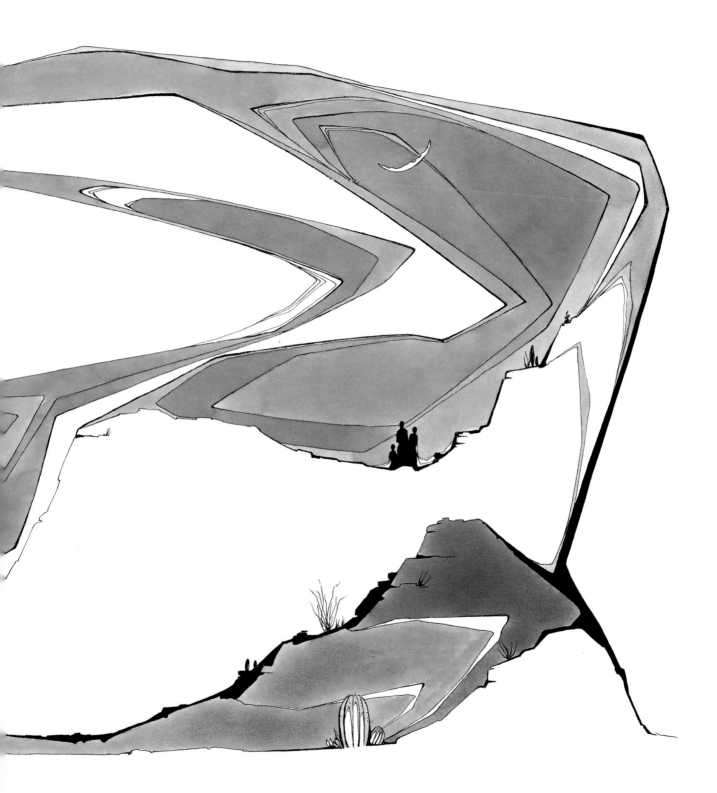

I kind of pat
the table
and I'm glad
it's ours.

In fact,
I think
the title of my book
is going to be
The Table Where Rich People Sit.